LONGMAN CLASSICS

The Count of Monte Cristo

Alexandre Dumas

Simplified by D K Swan
and Michael West

Longman

Longman Group UK Limited,
Longman House, Burnt Mill, Harlow,
Essex CM20 2JE, England
and Associated Companies throughout the world.

This simplified edition © Longman Group UK Limited 1989

First published 1989
Fourth impression 1992

ISBN 0-582-01820-X

Set in 10/13 point Linotron 202 Versailles
Printed in Hong Kong
SC/04

Acknowledgements

Photographs Courtesy of ITC Entertainments Limited

The cover background is a wallpaper design called NUAGE,
courtesy of Osborne and Little plc.

Stage 3:1300 word vocabulary

Please look under *New words* at the back of this book
for explanations of words outside this stage.

Contents

Introduction

Alexandre Dumas

There were two famous French writers, father and son, called Alexandre Dumas. The one who wrote *The Count of Monte Cristo* and very many other historical novels was Dumas *père*, the father. He was born in 1802. His father had been one of Napoleon's generals, but lost his post because of failure. When he died in 1806, there was very little money left for his family, so Alexandre's school education was not of much value.

At the age of sixteen he became a clerk, and he was lucky, after a time, to work for the Duke of Orleans. This work allowed him time to read a great deal. He became deeply interested in the plays of Shakespeare and the historical novels of Sir Walter Scott, and he himself began to write both plays and novels with a background of historical fact. The exciting happenings in his play *Henri III et sa cour* ("Henri III and his court"), seen in Paris in 1829, drew attention to the young writer. From then on, Dumas was able to spend all his time writing.

He is most famous, of course, for his historical novels (stories set in a real time in history). *The Three Musketeers* (1844) began a number of novels that covered about fifty years of French history in the seventeenth century. Several of them have given us well-known films such as *The Man in the Iron Mask* (from *Le Vicomte de Bragelonne*, 1848).

Another set of historical novels, the "Valois" novels,

had as background the sixteenth century in Europe.

In his own time, people spoke about Dumas' employment of other writers to help him with the very great number of books he wrote, but modern students of French literature have shown that most of the writing and all the stories were his own.

One reason for the very large number of books that came from his pen was the life he led. He spent a lot of money and enjoyed travel and adventure. One example of his love of adventure is his joining Garibaldi in Sicily in 1860, in a part of Garibaldi's fight to make Italy into the "one great country" that Faria dreams of in *The Count of Monte Cristo* (page 30).

The historical novels are nearly all long stories (we have made this English book much shorter than Dumas' novel in French), but the reader is taken at a good speed from one exciting moment to another. In modern times the novels have become films, radio and television plays and stories.

Dumas died in France in 1870.

The time of the story
This is a historical novel although the years of the action are in Dumas' own lifetime. The action begins in 1815, and the book appeared in 1844. In 1814, Napoleon had been sent to the island of Elba, which you will find on the map on page 39. He had been beaten by the Russian winter in 1812, and then by armies twice as big as his own at Leipzig in 1813. The forces against him had taken Paris in March 1814.

Napoleon was not a prisoner on Elba, although he was not allowed to leave the island. He controlled the government of Elba and brought in a number of good changes.

The victorious allies, Prussia, Russia, Britain, Austria, Sweden and some others, had brought back Bourbon kings to rule France, but most of the French people were not pleased with this arrangement. Napoleon knew about this feeling, and in 1815 he decided to return to France. He landed at Cannes on the first of March and moved through those parts of the country where his friends were, gathering the soldiers of his old armies as he went towards Paris. The king, Louis XVIII, left the country, and Napoleon entered Paris on the twentieth of March, beginning the "Hundred Days" which ended, after the battle of Waterloo, in Napoleon's being sent to the island of St Helena.

There is another historical person named in the book, Caesar (Cesare) Borgia. He was one of a family from Valencia in Spain (Spanish name: Borja) which became very powerful in Italy. Caesar Borgia, born in 1475, was the son of Rodrigo Borgia, who became Pope Alexander VI in 1492. As Faria's story in this book suggests, Caesar Borgia was ready to use any cruel way, including poison, to gain riches and power. When Caesar's father died, the new pope, Julius II, put Caesar in prison, but he escaped to Spain.

The Chateau d'If

This fearful-looking castle is still to be seen guarding the entrance to the Old Port of Marseilles. It is true that it was once used as a prison "for important persons, enemies of the king", as Edmond Dantes says on page 18. There are no prisoners there now. Tourists visit it because of the wonderful views from the top and because of the stories in The Count of Monte Cristo and other historical novels.

Chapter 1
The ship comes home

On the twenty-fourth of February 1815 the ship *Pharaoh* came in to Marseilles. A gentleman on shore jumped into a boat and was taken to meet the ship.

As the boat drew near, a young man came to the side of the ship. He seemed to be the captain. He was about twenty years of age. He had the quiet manner of one who meets danger without fear.

"Oh! Is it you, Dantes?" cried the man in the boat. "What has happened?"

"A very sad thing, Mr Morrel," replied the young man. "When our ship was near Civitavecchia we lost our brave Captain Leclerc."

Turning to his men, he gave a quick order. Then he turned again to Morrel. The *Pharaoh* was Morrel's ship, and Edmond Dantes had been First Officer after the captain.

"Well, Edmond," said Morrel, "we must all die some time. Now, the goods that the ship carries——?"

"They are all quite safe, Mr Morrel, and they are worth a lot of money. Now, if you will come on board, here is Danglars, who does all the buying and selling. I must look after my ship."

Morrel quickly climbed on board. He was met by Danglars.

Danglars was about twenty-five years of age. None of the men on board the *Pharaoh* liked him.

"Well, Mr Morrel," said Danglars, "you have heard of the sad death of Captain Leclerc?"

"Yes. He was a brave and good man."

1

Danglars and Morrel

"And a good seaman, old and wise, as a man should be if he works for Morrel and Son," replied Danglars.

"But a man need not always be old before he can understand his work. Our friend Edmond seems to know his work well."

"Yes," said Danglars, giving a look at Dantes which showed that he did not like him. "Yes – he is young, and he is very sure of himself. As soon as the captain was dead, he took command of the ship without asking anyone. And he caused us to lose a day and a half at the island of Elba instead of coming straight to Marseilles."

"Taking command of the ship," said Morrel, "was his duty because he was First Officer. It was wrong to lose time at Elba if the ship was safe and did not need any work done on it."

"The ship was in perfect condition, and the time was lost just for the pleasure of going on shore."

"Dantes," the ship owner called out, "come here, please."

"In a minute, Mr Morrel," answered Dantes. He gave an order to his men. The ship moved to its place and was safely tied up. When all was ready, Dantes came towards Morrel.

"The ship is now ready," he said, "and I am at your service."

Danglars took a few steps back.

"I wanted to ask you why you stopped at the island of Elba," said Morrel.

"I don't know, Mr Morrel. It was the last order that Captain Leclerc gave me. When he was near his death, he gave me a letter for Marshal Bertrand."

Morrel looked round him. Then he drew Dantes close to him and said quietly, "And how is Napoleon?"

3

"He seemed very well."

"You spoke to him?"

"No, it was he who spoke to me," said Dantes. "He asked me about the ship, about when it left Marseilles, and what goods it had on board. If the ship had had nothing on board and if I had been the owner, I believe he would have bought her. But I told him that I was only First Officer, and that Morrel and Son were the owners. 'Ah!' he said, 'I know them. The Morrels have been ship owners for many years. But there was a Morrel who was a soldier with me in the same company at Valence.'"

"True!" cried the delighted owner. "That was Policar Morrel, my uncle, later a captain in the army. Dantes, you must tell my uncle that Napoleon remembered him, and you will see it bring fire into the old soldier's eyes. – You were quite right, Dantes, to do as Captain Leclerc asked. But if people knew that you had taken a letter to Marshal Bertrand and had talked to Napoleon, it might get you into trouble."

"How?" asked Dantes. "I didn't even know what I was carrying, and Napoleon only asked me questions that he would have asked anyone."

"Well, my dear Dantes," asked the owner, "are you now free?"

"Yes, Mr Morrel."

"Then, can you come and have dinner with me?"

"Thank you, Mr Morrel, but my first visit must be to my father."

"Well, then, after you have made this first visit, I hope to see you."

"Thank you again, Mr Morrel, but after I have seen my father there is yet another person I must see."

"True, Dantes. I forgot that. Of course – the beautiful

4

Mercedes. She has come to me three times asking if I had any news about the *Pharaoh*. Edmond, you have a very beautiful lady-love."

"She is more than my lady-love now," the young seaman said. "She has promised to marry me."

"Well, well, my dear Edmond," said the owner, "I mustn't waste your time. Now hurry away to see your father."

"Thank you, Mr Morrel. – May I be allowed to leave my work for fourteen days?"

"To get married?"

"Yes, first. And then to go to Paris."

"Yes, of course. Take as much time as you need, Dantes. But you must be back again in a month because the *Pharaoh* can't sail without her captain."

"Without her captain!" cried Dantes, his eyes bright with joy. "Are you really going to make me captain of the *Pharaoh*? Oh, Mr Morrel!" he cried, "I thank you both for my father and for Mercedes."

"Good, Edmond. Go to your father, go and see Mercedes, and come to me afterwards."

"Shall I take you to the shore with me?"

"No, thank you. I'll stay and do some work with Danglars. Have you been pleased with him on this journey?"

"Do you mean, 'Is he a good friend?' No. I think he has never liked me since we had a quarrel one day near the island of Monte Cristo. If you mean, 'Did he do his work well?' – there is nothing against him."

The ship owner followed him with his eyes until he saw him reach the shore and mix with the crowd. Danglars stood behind, also watching the young man as he went away, but with a very different look.

Chapter 2
Father and son

Dantes turned into a narrow street and entered a small house.

"My dear Edmond," cried his father, "my boy, my son! I didn't expect you. Tell me all that has happened to you."

"The good Captain Leclerc is dead, and I am very sad about that. But Morrel tells me that I will be captain in his place. Do you understand, father? Just think! A captain at twenty years of age, with very good pay. Isn't that more than a poor seaman like me could have hoped for? With the first money I get, you will have a new house. – What's the matter, father? Aren't you well?"

"It's nothing. It will soon pass away."

"You need food, or something to drink. Where will I find it for you?"

"There's nothing in the house," answered the old man. "But I don't need anything, because you are here."

"I gave you plenty of money when I left, three months ago."

"Yes. You forget that we had to pay something back to our friend Caderousse. He asked me for it. He said that if I didn't pay, he would get the money from Mr Morrel. So – I gave it to him."

"But it was more than half the money that I gave you! So you have lived for three months on half of what I gave you. Why did you do that? Here, father, take this. Take it and send for some food at once."

He put all the money he had with him on the table.

"No, no," said the old man. "I don't need all that. – But here comes Caderousse. He has heard of your return and has come to tell you how pleased he is."

"Hullo! You've returned, Edmond?" Caderousse said.

"Yes, neighbour," replied Dantes, trying to hide his real feelings, "and ready to help you in any way."

"You've come back rich," said Caderousse, fixing a hungry look on the gold lying on the table.

"Oh that," said Dantes, seeing the look. "That's my father's money. But of course, if our neighbour wants any of it, we'll be glad to lend it."

"Thank you, thank you. But I don't need anything. I met my friend Danglars, and he told me you had returned. So I came to have the pleasure of meeting you."

"Good Caderousse!" said the old man. "He is such a friend to us."

There was a rather ugly look on Caderousse's face as he said, "Well, I hear that Morrel is pleased with you. You are hoping to be the next captain, perhaps?"

"Yes. I believe that I am to be the next captain. – But, dear father, now that I have seen you and know that you have all you need, I must go and pay another visit."

"Go, my dear boy. And may God bless your wife."

"His wife!" said Caderousse. "She isn't his wife yet. Mercedes is a fine girl, and fine girls have plenty of young fellows. But, as you will be captain——"

"No," Dantes answered. "I think better than you do of women – and of Mercedes. I am certain that, captain or not, she will always be true to me."

Edmond left the house. Caderousse went to join Danglars, who was waiting for him at the corner.

"He isn't captain yet," said Danglars quietly. "We can stop that if we wish. Let's go. We'll stop at La Reserve and drink a glass of wine there."

"Come on, then. But *you* must pay for the drink."

Chapter 3
Mercedes

Danglars and Caderousse sat at a table under a tree.

In one of the houses, about a hundred metres away, a young girl with hair as black as night, and eyes as dark and wonderful as the shadow of a forest, was standing near the wall.

"Mercedes!" a voice shouted cheerfully outside the house. "Mercedes!"

"Ah!" cried the girl. And she ran to the door and opened it, saying, "Here, Edmond, here I am!"

Edmond and Mercedes were in each other's arms. The golden sunshine of Marseilles shone round them like the light of heaven. They were alone with each other in the whole world.

Caderousse and Danglars were still at La Reserve when Edmond and Mercedes came past, walking side by side.

"Hey! Edmond," cried Caderousse, rising from his seat, "don't you see your friends? Or are you too proud to speak to them?"

"No, my dear fellow!" Dantes replied. "I'm not proud, but I'm happy. It was happiness that made me blind."

"Ah, well, that's a reason," said Danglars. "When is the marriage to be?"

"As soon as possible – tomorrow or the next day, here at La Reserve. We hope you and Caderousse will be there."

"Tomorrow or the next day! You are in a hurry, Captain," said Danglars.

"I'm not a captain yet, Danglars," said Dantes. "But,

yes, we are in a hurry because I must go to Paris."

"To Paris! Do you have business there?"

"Not of my own. When Captain Leclerc was dying, he asked me to do something for him."

"Yes, yes, I understand," said Danglars. And he added, speaking to himself, "To Paris – to take Marshal Bertrand's letter there, no doubt. Ah! A thought has come to me. Dantes, my friend, you certainly aren't captain of the *Pharaoh* yet!" He turned towards Edmond, who was walking away. "A good journey!" he cried.

"Thank you," said Edmond, in a friendly manner. And the two lovers continued on their joyful path.

"Boy," shouted Danglars, "bring me a pen and paper."

The things were brought.

"It's a strange thought," said Caderousse, "that that pen will kill a man more surely than if you waited for him at night with an axe!"

"I'll tell you what I am going to do," said Danglars. "Dantes has just come back from a journey during which he stopped at the island of Elba. We are going to send a letter to some officer of the government, saying that he is working for Napoleon, to bring Napoleon back as ruler of France instead of our present king."

Danglars wrote, using his left hand:

A friend of the king believes that the king's officers should know that Edmond Dantes, of the ship Pharaoh, brought with him from Elba a letter to the followers of Napoleon in Paris. The letter will be found with him, or at his father's house, or in his own room on the ship.

He put the letter in a cover and wrote a name on it: *Villefort*.

"So that's settled," he said.

"Yes, that's settled," said Caderousse. "But it's a dirty piece of work." He put out his hand to take the letter.

A wonderful meal had been prepared at La Reserve for the marriage. Many of the men from the *Pharaoh* were there, and other friends of Dantes, all in their best clothes.

Morrel arrived. The men of the *Pharaoh* understood from this that Dantes would be their next captain. Dantes was greatly loved by the men, so they cheered loudly.

"Shall we start?" asked the sweet silvery voice of Mercedes. "It is now two, and we are expected at the church in fifteen minutes."

The whole party rose up and began to form themselves into line.

There was the sound of a man striking the door – three times. "Open, in the name of the law!"

An officer entered, followed by four soldiers.

"Where is Edmond Dantes?"

"That is my name," said Edmond. "Why?"

"I cannot tell you. You will be told the reason later."

"Don't be afraid, my good friends," said Dantes. "This must be a mistake, and it will soon be put right. That's all, I'm sure."

"Of course," said Danglars. "Just a mistake, I'm sure."

Dantes went down to the courtyard, followed by the soldiers.

"God be with you, my dearest," cried Mercedes.

"And with you, sweet Mercedes. We'll soon meet again."

Chapter 4
The judge

Villefort, the judge, took a paper from one of the men and said, "Bring in the prisoner."

Dantes entered.

"Who and what are you?"

"My name is Edmond Dantes," the young man replied. "I am an officer of the *Pharaoh*, one of Morrel's ships."

"Your age?"

"Twenty."

"What were you doing at the time when you were made prisoner?"

"I was at my marriage." His voice broke. The thought of the change from that happiness was more than he could bear.

"At your marriage?" said Villefort.

"Yes. I was being married to a young girl I have loved for three years."

It made Villefort sad to hear this. But he went on.

"Have you served under Napoleon?"

"I was just going to join one of his ships when he fell from power."

"It is said that you are a dangerous man and wish to bring Napoleon back to power."

"*I*? Dangerous! I'm only twenty, and I don't know about such things or think about them. There are only three things that I think about: I love my father, I love Morrel, and above all I love Mercedes. That is all I can tell you."

"Have you any enemies?"

"Enemies?" said Dantes. "I'm not important enough to

Villefort

have enemies. I have ten or twelve sailors under me, but if you ask them they will tell you that they love me – not as a father, because I am too young – but as an elder brother."

"You will soon be made a captain, at the age of only twenty. You are marrying a pretty girl who loves you. Perhaps someone is your enemy because of that."

"You may be right. You know men better than I do."

"This is the paper that I received. Do you know the writing?"

Dantes read it, and a cloud of sadness passed over his face.

"No. I don't know the writing. But it is clear that this man is a real enemy."

Villefort saw in Dantes' eyes what strength lay behind those gentle words.

"Now," said the judge, "answer me, not as a prisoner to a judge, but as one man to another: what truth is there in this paper?"

"None at all. I'll tell you the facts. Captain Leclerc fell ill soon after we left Naples. On the third day he was very ill and he felt that death was near. He called me and said, 'Promise that you will do what I tell you. It's a very important matter.' I promised. 'After my death, you will become captain. Go to Elba and ask for Marshal Bertrand. Give him this letter, and perhaps he will give you another letter and tell you where to take it. You will then do what I should have done if I had been alive.'"

"And what did you do then?"

"I did what I was asked to do – what everyone would have done in my place. It is a man's duty to listen to the wishes of someone on his death-bed, but among seamen the last wishes of an officer are commands. I reached Elba. I went on shore alone. I gave the letter to Marshal

Bertrand, and he gave me a letter to take to a person in Paris. I came here, visited Mercedes, and prepared for the marriage. I was at my marriage party. I was going to start for Paris tomorrow."

"Ah," said Villefort, "you seem to be telling the truth. If you have done wrong, it was because you were unwise, and that was caused by the orders of your captain. Give up this letter that you brought from Elba, promise to appear before me again if I call you, and you can go back to your friends."

"I am free, then?" said Dantes joyfully.

"Yes, but first give me the letter."

"You have it already. It was taken from me with some other letters that I see there on the table."

"Stop," said Villefort, as Dantes took his hat. "What name was written on the letter?"

"Noirtier, Heron Road, Paris."

If the roof had fallen down, Villefort could not have been more surprised.

"Noirtier!" he said in a weak voice. "Noirtier!"

"Yes. Do you know him?"

"No," replied Villefort, "a true servant of the king does not know men who wish to destroy the king's power and to bring back Napoleon."

"Is that what they want to do?" Dantes began to feel afraid. "I have told you that I know nothing about what is in the letter."

"Yes, but you know the name of the person it is addressed to."

"Of course. I read the name so as to know who to give it to."

"Have you shown this letter to anyone?" asked Villefort, his face white as death.

"To no one. I give you my word."

The look on Villefort's face filled Dantes with fear. Villefort read the letter, then he covered his face with his hands. "Oh!" the judge thought. "If he knows what is in this letter. If he knows that I have changed my name and that Noirtier is my father, then I am lost!"

Villefort fixed his eyes on Dantes as if he wanted to read his thoughts. Then he said: "I can't, as I had hoped, set you free at once. I must keep you for a time. I'll try to make it as short as possible. The only thing against you is this."

He took the letter from the table, and went to the fire. "Look, I'm burning it."

"Oh," cried Dantes, "you are very kind."

"Listen," said Villefort. "You can trust me after what I have just done. You will be kept here until this evening. If anyone else questions you, don't say a word about this letter, and don't say the name of Noirtier."

"I promise."

"It was the only letter you had?"

"Yes."

Villefort rang his bell. A soldier entered.

"Follow him," said Villefort to Dantes.

As soon as the door closed, Villefort threw himself into a chair. "Oh, my father, must you always stand in the way of my happiness? If this letter had become known, it would have been the end for me. I must make sure – very sure – that it will never be known!"

Chapter 5
The prison

Dantes was taken to a small room.

Evening came. He sat in the darkness, but at every little sound he rose and hurried to the door.

At about ten, an officer and four soldiers took him through many streets to the shore. There were more soldiers here. They looked at Dantes curiously as he was placed in a boat. The boat moved off.

Strange and wild thoughts passed through Edmond's mind. The boat they were in could not go on any long journey. Perhaps they were going to leave him at some distant point on the shore. The judge had been so kind to him, had told him that he had nothing to fear if he did not say the name Noirtier, and had destroyed the letter in front of him.

Dantes looked into the darkness. They were going out to sea, away from everything that was dear to him.

At last he turned to the nearest soldier.

"Friend," he said, "please tell me where we are going. I am Edmond Dantes, a seaman, and a man true to God and the king. Tell me where you are taking me."

"You were born in Marseilles, and you are a seaman, and you don't know where you are going? Look!"

Dantes stood up and looked forward. Less than a hundred metres away he saw the black and fearful shape of the rock on which the Chateau d'If stands. The prison was about three hundred years old. Many strange stories were told about it and about prisoners who went there and never came back. To Dantes it seemed the end of all hope.

Edmond is taken to the Chateau d'If

"The Chateau d'If!" Dantes cried. "What are we going there for?"

The soldier laughed.

"I'm not going to be a prisoner there?" said Dantes. "It's only used for important prisoners, enemies of the king. Are there any judges at the Chateau d'If?"

"The judge has seen you and questioned you."

"But Mr Villefort promised me——"

"I don't know what Mr Villefort promised, but I do know that we are taking you to Chateau d'If."

The boat reached the shore. A soldier jumped out, and they took his arms and forced him to go up some steps. He was like a man in a dream. He passed through a door, and the door closed behind him, but he saw all this as if through a cloud.

They stopped. He tried to think. He looked round. He was in a courtyard with high walls on all sides. He heard the feet of soldiers marching about on guard.

"Where is the prisoner?" a voice said. "Follow me."

Dantes followed, and the man led him to a room almost under the ground. Water ran down its walls in great drops, like tears. A lamp threw a dim light around and showed him the face of the prison-keeper who had brought him there.

"This is your room for tonight," the man said. "It's late, and the governor is asleep. Tomorrow, perhaps, he may put you somewhere else. There's bread and water – and some dry grass to sleep on. Good night."

Before Dantes could open his mouth to speak, before he had noticed where the man had put the bread and water, before he had looked towards the corner where his bed was, the man had gone, taking the lamp with him.

Dantes was alone in darkness and in silence.

At the first light of day the keeper returned with orders that Dantes was to remain where he was. He found the prisoner just as he had left him. He had passed the night standing and without sleep.

The man drew near. Dantes appeared not to notice him. He touched him on the arm and asked, "Haven't you slept?"

"I don't know," Dantes answered.

The keeper looked at him. "Are you hungry?"

"I don't know."

"Do you want anything?"

"I want to see the governor."

The man gave a short laugh, and left the room.

Dantes held out his hands towards the open door, but the door closed. Then his feelings were too strong. He threw himself on the floor, weeping and asking himself what he had done to be treated like this.

The day passed. He did not eat any food, but walked round and round like a beast in its cage.

The next morning the keeper appeared again.

"Well," he said, "are you feeling better today?" Dantes made no reply.

"Be brave, man. Is there anything I can do for you?"

"I want to see the governor."

"That isn't allowed."

"What is allowed, then?"

"Better food – if you pay for it – books, and to walk about in the yard."

"I don't want books. This food is good enough. And I don't want to walk about. But I want to see the governor."

"Don't keep on asking for what you can't have, or you'll be mad in a month."

"You think so?"

"I know it. We've got a man here who was always offering some great treasure to the governor if he would set him free. He was in this room before you."

"How long ago did he leave it?"

"Two years."

"Was he set free then?"

"No. He was put in a room underground."

"Listen. I'm not mad. Perhaps I'm going to be, but at present I'm not. And I must see the governor."

"Oh, ho!" cried the man, stepping back. "You are certainly going mad. The other fellow began like that. In three days we will have trouble with you. But there are those places underground."

There was a chair near Dantes. He raised it above his head.

"Oh!" said the keeper. "You shall see the governor at once."

He went out, and soon afterwards returned with four soldiers.

"By the governor's orders," he said, "take this prisoner to the room just under this one."

"To that underground place?" said one of the soldiers.

"Yes. We must put madmen with madmen."

The soldiers took hold of Dantes. He went quietly. They went down fifteen steps. The door of a room was opened, and he was thrown in.

The door closed, and Dantes walked forward, holding his hands out until he touched the wall. Then he sat down in a corner until his eyes became used to the darkness.

The keeper was right: Dantes was not very far from being completely mad.

Chapter 6
Underground

Time passed, and a visit was made by the chief officer of prisons.

The officer visited the rooms of several of the prisoners – those that the governor favoured because they gave no trouble. He asked how they were fed, and if they wanted anything. They all answered that the food was very bad, and that they wanted to be set free. The officer asked if they wanted anything else. They said "No." What could they want except to be set free?

The officer laughed and turned to the governor. "I don't know what reason the government has for these visits. It's always the same thing: 'The food is bad. I have done nothing wrong: set me free.' Are there any others?"

"Yes, there are the mad and dangerous prisoners."

"Let's visit them. I must see them all."

Two soldiers were sent for, and the officer went down the steps. The air was fearful. The darkness seemed to be full of the smell of death.

"Oh!" cried of officer. "Who can live here?"

"A very dangerous man that we are ordered to watch most carefully."

This was the officer's first visit. He wanted to show what a great man he was.

"Number thirty-four. Let's visit this one first," he said.

At the sound of the key turning, Dantes, who was sitting in a corner, raised his head. He saw the stranger with two soldiers, and he noticed that the governor stood with his hat off. He knew then that this must be some high officer, and he sprang to meet him.

The soldiers stepped forward and forced him back. Dantes saw that the officer had been told that he was a dangerous man. Making his eyes and voice as gentle as possible, he spoke to the officer and tried to move his heart. He ended: "I ask only to know what wrong I am supposed to have done, and to see a judge, and to know what is to happen to me."

"We shall see," said the officer. Then, turning to the governor, he said, "You must show me what there is against this poor fellow in your books."

"I know you can't set me free," said Dantes, "but tell me at least that there is hope."

"I can't tell you that. I can only promise to ask about the matter. Who gave orders for you to be taken prisoner?"

"Mr Villefort."

"Did he have any reason to be your enemy?"

"None. He was very kind to me."

"Then I can trust anything that he has written about you?"

"Yes."

The door was closed. But there was something in the room which had not been there before – hope.

The officer kept his promise to Dantes. He looked in the prison book and found:

EDMOND DANTES
A dangerous man. Helped the return of Napoleon from Elba.
To be watched with the greatest possible care.

The officer could do nothing about such a prisoner. He just wrote: *"Nothing to be done."*

Chapter 7
Number Twenty-seven

Days and weeks passed, and Dantes began to think that the visit of the officer had been only a dream.

Suddenly one evening, at about nine, Edmond heard a sound in the wall beside which he was lying. He raised his head and listened. Perhaps it was only a dream, he thought. But no, he still heard the sound. Then he heard the noise of something falling – and then silence.

Some hours after that, it began again, nearer and more clearly. Dantes was afraid the keeper might hear the noise and put an end to his last touch of hope.

When the keeper brought him his breakfast, Dantes began to talk about everything: about the bad food, the cold room, speaking loudly and angrily. The keeper put the food down on the table and went away.

Edmond listened, and the sounds became louder and clearer.

"There's no doubt about it," he thought. "It's a prisoner trying to escape."

Full of joy at discovering this, Edmond wanted to help. He began by moving his bed. Then he looked round the room for something to use to cut away at the wall and take a stone out of its place. All that was in the room was a bed, a chair, a table, and a water pot. There was only one thing to do, and that was to break the water pot and use one of the pointed bits. He threw the pot on the floor, and it broke into pieces. He hid two or three of the most pointed bits in his bed.

When the keeper came the next morning, he told him that the water pot had fallen from his hands when he was drinking. The man was angry with him for his careless-ness, but he brought another, and he did not take away the broken pieces of the old one.

Dantes started to work. The wall was soft with age. It came away, in small pieces. Working as quickly as this, he might in his two years have made an underground passage six metres long and half a metre wide.

"Why," he asked himself, "did I waste all those hours in weeping?"

At last he got a stone out from the wall. It left a hole half a metre across. He carefully gathered together all the dust and dirt, carried it into the corners of the room, and covered it with earth. He put back the stone, and put his bed back to hide it before the keeper came with his even-ing meal. As soon as the man had gone, he started to work again, and continued all night, digging his way far into the wall. Then he came to a stop. There was some-thing in his way that he could neither cut nor move. It was wood. A great piece of wood crossed the hole that Dantes had made, completely stopping the way.

"Oh, my God, my God!" he cried. "Let me die. I have lost all hope."

"Who talks of God and yet has lost all hope?" said a voice under the earth – like a voice from the grave.

Edmond rose on his knees. "Ah!" he said, "a voice – the voice of a man!" He had heard no one speak since he came to the prison, except the governor and the officer and his keeper. And the keeper is not a man to a prisoner. He is a living door.

"In the name of heaven," cried Dantes, "speak again."

"Who are you?" said the voice.

"An unhappy prisoner."

"Why are you in prison?"

Edmond hides the hole in the wall

"I did nothing wrong."

"What are you supposed to have done?"

"To have tried to help Napoleon return to France."

"To return! Is he no longer in France, then?"

"He was sent to the island of Elba in 1814. How long have you been here, if you do not know that?"

"Since 1811."

"Four years longer than I have been here!"

"Don't do any more work," said the voice. "Just tell me how high up you are."

"In a line with the floor of my room."

"How is the opening hidden?"

"By my bed."

"Where does the door of your room open?"

"In a passage leading into the courtyard."

"Oh! That's bad. I was wrong. I'm five metres out of the line of my plan. I mistook the wall where you are working for the outside wall of the prison."

"And if you had made your way through?"

"I should have thrown myself into the sea and tried to swim to one of the islands near here."

"Can you swim so far?"

"God would have given me strength. But now there's nothing to hope for."

"Nothing?"

"Nothing. Stop up the opening of the hole you have made. Do it carefully. Don't work any more. Wait until you hear from me."

"Tell me at least who you are," cried Edmond.

"I'm – I'm Number Twenty-seven."

"You don't trust me, then?"

Edmond thought he heard a laugh.

"Oh!" he cried, afraid that the man did not want to talk

to him again, "I promise that I won't say a word – not one word – to the keepers. But please – please don't leave me alone."

"All right," said the voice. "Tomorrow."

Edmond moved back. He closed the opening in the wall, carefully hid the bits that he had cut out, and put his bed back in its place.

The next morning, just as he moved his bed away from the wall, he heard a sound. He got down on his knees.

"Is it you?" he said. "I'm here."

"Has your keeper gone?"

"Yes. He won't return until the evening."

"I can work, then."

Soon after that, the floor on which Dantes' two hands were resting fell away. He threw himself back while a lot of stones and earth went down into the opening. Then, from the bottom of the hole (he could not tell how deep it was), the arms and head of a man appeared. He climbed up into the room.

Dantes reached his hands out to the friend he had wanted for so long, and almost carried him towards the window so as to see his face better in the light.

He was a small man, his hair white with suffering rather than age. His eyes were deep-set, and he had a long beard. It seemed as if he had no great strength of body: he appeared to be a man who worked with his mind rather than with his hands. The warm manner in which Dantes received him seemed to move his heart. He thanked Edmond for his kindness, though he must have been suffering greatly at finding another room where he had hoped to find the free and open air.

"Let's first see," he said, "whether it's possible to hide

The two prisoners meet

28

these marks here. We must make sure that the keeper won't discover our hidden passage." He went to the opening, took the stone in his hands and picked it up as if its weight was nothing. Then, fitting it into its place, he said, "You took this stone out rather carelessly. What did you use for the work?"

Dantes showed him the pieces of the water pot.

"Oh," he said, "I have better instruments than those. I made them out of pieces of my bed. With them I have cut a path at least six metres long. That's the distance between your room and mine. But I didn't draw my plan right. The passage I have made would only take me into the courtyard, which is full of soldiers."

"You have reached this room. There are three other sides to it. Couldn't we cut a way under one of these three walls? Do you know what is outside them?"

"One is built against the rock. Nothing can be done there. One wall is against the lower part of the governor's house. If we got there, we would certainly be caught. And this side looks out – where?"

The side they were looking at was the one that had a small window. It was very high up in the wall, so small that only a child could have got through it, even if three strong bars had not been added to make it even harder.

Pulling the table across the room, the newcomer set it up under the window. Then he asked Dantes to climb on it, put his back against the wall, and join his hands in front of him. Then "Number Twenty-seven" jumped up on to the table, and from there on to Dantes' hands, and from them on to Dantes' shoulders. He put his head through the top bars of the window so as to see the whole wall outside. He drew his head back quickly, saying, "I thought so." Then he got down as quickly and as easily as he had got up. Dantes was surprised at the quickness of so old a man.

"This side of your room," said Number Twenty-seven, "looks out onto a kind of open pathway where a soldier keeps watch day and night. I saw the top of the soldier's head. That was what made me draw back so quickly. I was afraid he might see me."

"Well?" said Dantes.

"Well, you see, then, that it is not possible to escape through any of these walls."

Dantes looked with wonder at this person who could so quickly and so quietly give up the hope that had strengthened him for years.

"Tell me, please," he said at last, "who you are."

"Certainly," replied the other. "My name is Faria. I have been a prisoner in the Chateau d'If since the year 1811. Before that, I was three years in the prison of Fenestrelle."

"But why are you here?"

"Italy is, as you know, broken up into a number of small separate countries, each with its own separate ruler. My wish was to make it one great country under one great king. I thought that I had found that great king, but he was only a fool. He listened to me only so that he could learn my plans and destroy me. And now perhaps that great work will never be done. Napoleon began to make Italy one country, but he was unable to complete his work. Italy has not been lucky." The old man said these last words with deep sadness.

"I'd like to see the passage you have made."

"Follow me, then," said Faria, and he entered the underground passage, and was soon out of sight.

Dantes followed.

Chapter 8
Faria's room

The two friends passed quite easily along the underground path. Faria raised a stone in the floor, and they climbed up into his room.

As he entered the room, Dantes looked around with wonder, but he noticed nothing uncommon. "There is one thing that I still don't understand," he said, "and that is how you found time to do so much by daylight."

"I work at night, too."

"At night? Are your eyes like cat's eyes? Can you see in the dark?"

"No, of course not. But God has given man a mind so that he can supply his needs. I made a lamp for myself."

"You did! But tell me, how did you get oil for the lamp?"

"I get the oil from my food, and it burns very well. This is my lamp." He showed it to Dantes.

They sat and talked. Faria's words were full of learning and wisdom. Dantes listened to him in wonder. Sometimes he spoke of things well known to Dantes as a seaman. Sometimes Edmond could not understand the things he spoke of at all.

"Will you teach me a small part of what you know," Dantes asked, "so that you will not become tired of me? I can well believe that a learned person like yourself would be as happy to be alone as to be sitting with a person who knows almost nothing. But, if I am ready to learn and you to teach, then the hours might pass more easily for you."

Dantes had a quick understanding and, having once learnt a thing, he never forgot it. He learnt from Faria

31

very quickly and easily. He learnt the history of the world, and English, and many other things.

Time passed. Dantes became a new man. But Faria's health was clearly failing.

One day, Faria was in Edmond's room while Edmond was at work on the passage between their rooms. Suddenly Edmond heard him cry out in pain. He hurried up to him, and found him standing in the middle of the room, his face white as death.

"What's the matter?" cried Dantes.

"Quick!" replied Faria. "Listen to what I have to say."

Dantes looked in fear and wonder at Faria's face. His eyes were dim, and round them were deep blue circles. His skin was like the skin of a dead man.

"Listen," said Faria. "I have a fearful illness which may end in my death. I can feel it coming over me fast. I had an illness of the same kind about a year before I was put in prison. There is only one thing to do. Help me back to my room while I have some strength. Take out one of the feet which hold up my bed, and you will find a hole in it. The hole contains a small jar full of red liquid."

Dantes was used to dealing with sudden dangers. While the old man was still talking, he quickly pulled him down into the underground passage, and into Faria's room, where he laid him on the bed.

"Thank you," the poor man said. He was as cold now as if his blood had been frozen. "Now I must tell you about this illness. When it reaches its height, I lie without moving and become as cold as death. Then – and not before – force open my mouth and pour eight or ten drops of the liquid into it. And perhaps I will be well again."

He could say no more. Across his face came the fearful greyness of death.

Dantes waited until life seemed to have left the body of his friend. Then, taking Faria's knife, he forced open the mouth and poured in nine drops of the liquid. Then he waited, in fear, to see what would happen.

One hour went by, and there was no change, no beginning of the return to life. Then at last a little colour seemed to come. The dim, wide-open eyes appeared to show some life. And then he tried to move. He was not yet able to speak, but he pointed to the door, and there was fear in his eyes. Dantes listened, and heard clearly the steps of the keeper. Edmond's fear had driven all thought of time from his mind.

The young man sprang to the opening of the underground passage. He put the stone over the opening and hurried to his own room. Just after he reached it, the door opened and the keeper entered, and saw his prisoner sitting as usual on the side of his bed.

Dantes left untouched the food which the keeper had brought. As soon as the key had turned, he hurried back to Faria's room. He raised the stone by pressing his head against it, and was soon beside the sick man's bed.

Faria now knew where he was, and he could speak, but he was still very weak.

"Don't lose hope," said Dantes. "Your strength will return." And as he spoke, he sat down on the bed beside Faria and rubbed the old man's cold hands.

"No," said Faria. "My first illness lasted for only half an hour. When it ended, I felt hungry – nothing else. I rose from my bed without help. Now I can't move my right arm or leg, and there is a pain in my head. The next of these illnesses will kill me."

33

Chapter 9
The story of the treasure

When Dantes returned to Faria's room next morning, he found Faria looking a little better. At first he did not speak, but he showed Dantes a small piece of paper.

Edmond took it. Half of it had been burnt away. He said, "I can't see anything except broken lines and words which don't hold together to give any meaning, and aren't easy to read because of the burning."

"I have found the meaning. But first listen to the history of this paper.

"You know," said Faria, "that I was the friend and helper of Prince Spada, the last of the princes of that name. I was very happy with him. He was not rich, although his family had at one time been famous for its riches. Indeed, there is a common saying: 'As rich as a Spada'. But he had very little money.

"I had often seen the prince studying old books and looking among the papers of the family. One day he told me about the Spada who lived – and died – at the time of the evil Caesar Borgia.

"Caesar Borgia needed money for his wars. It was not easy at that time to get money because the long wars had left the country in a very bad condition. At last he thought of a plan. There were two men, Rospigliosi and Spada, who were well known for their riches. Caesar Borgia asked them to dinner. The table was set ready in his garden. Rospigliosi was delighted at the honour, and he put on his best clothes. Spada was a wise man. He knew what this dinner meant: it meant certain death. Before he left, he wrote a note. At dinner he knew that there was

On May 25th 1498, I was
Caesar Borgia. I fear that
so that he may get all my
those of Prince Capra and
I desire that all I have
my death to Guido Spada
in a place he knows of, and
that is, on the island of Monte
gold, money, jewels, I have
the twenty-second rock from
bay to the east. There steps
leading down underground
into the second room: the
in the north-east cor

Caesar

May

death in the glass at his side. But there was also death if he did not drink. Spada drank – and died.

"Caesar Borgia then took everything. He took all the dead man's papers, and the paper he had written just before his death:

I give to my brother's child all that I have, all my money and all my books, and, among the books, my prayer book with the gold corners. I hope that he will keep this prayer book carefully, and that it will help him to remember his uncle.

"Caesar looked everywhere, but he discovered nothing. There were some gold cups and a few jewels, a little money – very little – and that was all. The treasure of the Spadas, if there ever was any, had gone.

"In the end, Caesar Borgia was driven away from Rome. People thought that now the treasure of the Spadas would appear again. But that did not happen. The Spadas remained poor, and people said that perhaps Caesar Borgia really had found the money.

"Years went by. I come now to the last of the Spadas, the man who was my friend, Prince Spada.

"The famous prayer book remained in the family, and the Prince now had it.

"Like many before me, I went through all the papers of the family – rooms full of papers – trying to find the answer to the old question: 'Where is the treasure of the Spadas?' I found nothing. I read through all the history of the Borgia family to discover whether Caesar Borgia ever got the money. I found that he certainly got all the riches of Rospigliosi, but I could find nothing about the riches of the Spadas. At last I was quite sure that the treasure had remained hidden all this time.

"My friend died. At his death, all that he had came to me. In leaving it to me, he asked only that I would write a history of the Spada family.

"In 1807, a month before I became a prisoner, I was reading some papers when I fell asleep.

"It was evening when I woke up. Everything was dark except for the dim firelight. I took the lamp in one hand, and with the other hand I felt about for a piece of paper so as to get a light from the fire. I didn't want to burn any important papers, but I remembered that there was a piece of plain white paper in the prayer book. It had been used to mark the reader's place in the book, and it had been there for very many years. I took it and put a corner in the fire. As the fire spread up the paper, yellow writing began to appear. I put out the fire as quickly as I could. I opened the paper and looked at it. Words had been written on the paper in a liquid which would appear only when the paper was heated. A part of the paper had already been destroyed by fire.

"That paper in your hands is what remains."

Dantes looked again at the yellow writing.

"And now," said Faria, "look at this." And he gave Dantes a second piece of paper with broken lines of writing on it. "Put the two pieces together. – Do you understand now?"

"Yes. But the writing on the second piece is different."

"It's my writing," said Faria. "That's my completion of the old paper. When I had made it, I decided to set out at once, taking with me the beginnings of my great book about Italy. But the government were already afraid of me. They couldn't understand why I wanted to go away so suddenly. I was taken prisoner just as I was going on board the ship."

On May 25th 1498, I was asked to dinner by
Caesar Borgia. I fear that he will kill me
so that he may get all my riches as he did get
those of Prince Capra and Bentivoglio.
I desire that all I have shall pass after
my death to Guido Spada. I have hidden it
in a place he knows of, and has visited with me
that is, on the island of Monte Cristo. All my
gold, money, jewels, I have hidden there. Raise
the twenty-second rock from the shore of the small
bay to the east. There steps will be found
leading down underground. Break through
into the second room: the treasure is
in the north-east corner of it.

Caesar Spada
May 25th 1498

Faria looked at Dantes in the way a father looks at his child.

"And now, my dear fellow," he said, "you know as much as I do myself. If we ever escape together, half this treasure is yours. If I die here and you escape alone, the whole of it is yours."

"The treasure is yours, dear friend," said Dantes, "and yours only. I have no right to it. I am not one of your family."

"You are my son, Edmond," cried the old man. "You are my child, born to me in this prison. God has sent you to be a joy to a man who could not be a father and who could not be free."

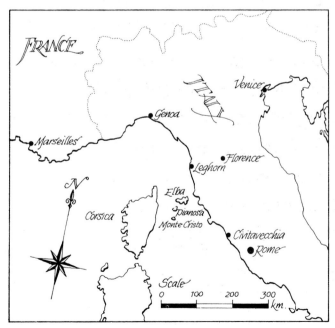

Chapter 10
The death of Faria

"Thank you," said the young man to Faria. "But neither of us will have the treasure, because neither of us will leave this prison. My real treasure is the teaching you give me, the wisdom I have learned from you and the joy of talking to you for five or six hours each day."

So, if they were not really happy, yet the days passed quickly – and not unhappily. Faria still talked about his treasure, and he was always thinking about ways of escape for his young friend. For fear that the letter would be lost, he made Dantes learn it word by word, and he burnt the paper on which he had written the words that completed the meaning.

Faria had not got back the use of his arm and leg, but all the clearness of his understanding had returned to him. He continued to teach Dantes history and English and other subjects, and he also taught him – as the first duty of a prisoner – to make something out of nothing. So they were always busy. Faria kept himself busy so that he would not see himself grow old. Dantes worked so as not to remember the past.

One night, Edmond awoke suddenly. His name – or rather, a weak voice trying to say his name – came to him through the darkness.

He moved his bed, took out the stone, and hurried along the underground passage. The other end of it was open. By the weak light of Faria's lamp he saw the old man, white faced, holding on to the end of his bed. On his face was that fearful pain that Dantes already knew.

"Ah, my dear friend," said Faria, "you understand, don't you? I needn't tell you. The time has come for me to die."

"Oh, my friend," cried Dantes, "don't say that! I've saved you once. I'll save you again."

He quickly raised the foot of the bed and took out the little jar. There was still some of the red liquid in it.

"Look," he cried. "There's still some left. Tell me what I must do this time."

"There isn't a hope," Faria replied. "But it is right that you should do all that you can to save a life. Do as you did before, but don't wait so long. Give me twelve drops. Then, if I don't get better, pour the rest into my mouth. Now put me on my bed."

Edmond took the old man in his arms and laid him on the bed.

"Dear friend," said Faria, "and joy of my life, you that heaven gave me rather late – but gave me, and I am thankful. If you escape, go to Monte Cristo. Take the treasure and enjoy it. Enjoy it because you have indeed suffered long enough. God be with you!" And he fell back on his bed.

Dantes waited, holding the jar of liquid in his hand. The uncertain lamplight filled the room with strange dancing shadows. When he believed the right time had come, he poured twelve drops into Faria's mouth, and waited. The jar still contained perhaps twelve drops. He waited – ten minutes – half an hour. Then he put the jar to Faria's mouth and poured in all that was left.

Faria moved. His eyes opened. He gave a little cry. Then silence.

Half an hour – an hour – an hour and a half passed, and still Edmond sat with his hand over Faria's heart.

41

The heart became weaker and weaker. And then the body slowly became cold.

Dantes went down into the underground passage, closing it after him as well as he could.

He was just in time: the keeper was coming. He came first to Dantes' room, and then he went on to Faria's room to take his breakfast and some clothes.

Dantes felt then that he must know what was happening in his friend's room. He went down the underground passage and arrived just in time to hear the keeper cry out.

Other keepers came. Dantes could hear them talking.

"Well, well," one of them said, "the madman has gone to look after his treasure. A good journey to him!"

"And with all his money, he won't have enough to pay for a grave-cloth!"

"Oh, the grave-cloth of the Chateau d'If doesn't cost much. A simple bag – of plain cloth. That will be all he'll get."

Edmond heard every word, but he understood very little of what they said. Then there was silence, as if they had gone away. He still didn't dare to enter: they might have left someone to watch.

At the end of an hour he heard a noise. The governor had come, and there was someone with him.

"Yes," said an unknown voice, "he's certainly dead."

"I don't doubt that," the governor said, "but by the rules of the prison we must check. We must be perfectly certain that the prisoner is dead."

There was a short silence. Someone was looking at and touching the body.

"You may be quite sure," said the voice. "He is dead.

There is no question of that."

More footsteps were heard, going and coming. Then there was the sound of some large piece of cloth being pulled along the floor. There was a sound from the bed, then the heavy feet of a man moving as if he were lifting a weight. Then another sound from the bed as a weight was laid on it.

"In the evening," said the governor.

"At what time?" asked the keeper.

"About ten or eleven."

"Shall we watch by the body?"

"No. That isn't necessary. Lock the door as if he were alive – that's all."

The steps went away. The voices died into the distance. There was the sound of a door being locked. Then there was silence, the deepest of all silences – the silence of death.

Dantes raised the stone with his head. He looked carefully round the room. There was no one there.

He went in.

Chapter 11
The grave of the Chateau d'If

On the bed Dantes saw, in the dim light, a long bag made
of yellow cloth. Inside it lay the body of his friend Faria.
This was the grave-cloth which, as the keeper had said,
cost so little.

Dantes and his old friend were separated. He could no
longer see those eyes which had remained open as if to
look even beyond death. He sat on the edge of the bed as
the sad thought passed through his mind.

"Alone! I am alone again."

As he said this he stopped, his eyes fixed. A strange
thought had come to him.

"Who sent me that strange thought? Was it God
himself? Or ..? *Since none but the dead ever leave this
prison, let me take the place of the dead.*"

He did not give himself more time to think about it. It
had to be done at once. He opened the bag with the knife
that Faria had made. He took the body from it and carried
it along the underground passage to his own room. He
laid it on his bed and drew the bedclothes over its head
just as he drew them himself when he was lying there. He
laid one kiss on the cold face, then turned the face
towards the wall so that the keeper, when he brought the
evening meal, would believe he was asleep.

He returned to the other room. He took from its
hiding-place one of the needles that Faria and he had
made. He took off his clothes and hid them. Then he got
inside the bag, and placed himself in just the same way as
the dead body had been laid, and joined up the mouth of
the bag from inside.

Edmond inside the bag

Now his plan was settled, whatever happened. While they were carrying him, the men might discover that they were carrying a living man instead of a dead body. If that happened, he planned to open the bag from top to bottom with a sudden cut of the knife, and to escape before they got over their surprise. If they tried to catch him, he would use the knife.

When they laid him in the grave, he planned to let them cover him with earth. It would be night, and he expected to be able to work his way through the soft soil almost as soon as they had gone away. He only hoped that the weight of the earth would not be too great for him.

The first danger was that the keeper, bringing his evening meal at seven, might notice the change that he had made. But luckily, Dantes had often – twenty times at least – been in bed when the man came, and then the man had put the food on the table and gone away without saying a word.

This time the keeper might not be as silent as usual. He might speak to Dantes and, getting no answer, go to the bed, and so discover everything.

But the hours passed and all was quiet in the prison. Dantes felt that he had escaped his first danger.

At last, at about the time that the governor had fixed, Edmond heard footsteps outside. The time had come. He must be brave now, braver than ever in his life before. They stopped at the door. There were two of them, he decided. He heard them put down some wooden thing that they were going to carry the body on.

The door opened, and a dim light reached his eyes through the cloth of the bag. He saw two shadows come near to his bed. Another man remained at the door with the lamp. One man came to each end of the bag.

"He's heavy for a thin old man," one of them said, as he raised the head.

"They say that every year adds something to the weight of the bones," said the other, lifting the feet.

"Have you tied it on?" the first speaker asked.

"What would be the use of carrying so much unnecessary weight?" was the reply. "I can do that when we get there."

"Yes, I suppose you're right."

" 'Tied it on' – tied *what* on?" thought Dantes.

They put the "dead" body on the carrier. Then the party moved up the steps.

Suddenly Dantes felt the cold and fresh night air. The men went forward about twenty metres, then stopped and put the body down.

One of them went away. Dantes heard the sound of his shoes on the stone.

"Where am I?" he asked himself.

"He really is a heavy load!" said the other man, sitting down on the edge of the carrier.

For a minute Dantes thought of making his escape now. But luckily he did not try to do so.

"Give me some light, you," said the other fellow, "or I won't find what I'm looking for."

The man with the lamp moved towards the voice.

"What can he be looking for?" Dantes wondered. "Is it something to make the grave with? But surely the grave must be ready?"

"Here it is. I've found it."

The man came towards Edmond. He heard some heavy object laid down beside him. Then something was tied round his feet.

"Is that tied strongly enough?" asked the man who was watching.

"Yes. That won't come off, I can tell you," was the answer.

"Move off, then."

Dantes felt himself lifted up again, and they moved some steps forward. They stopped to open a door, then forward again. Now the sound of waves beating against the rocks came clearly to his ears.

"Well, here we are at last," said one of the men.

"A little farther," said the other, "a little farther. You know very well that the last one didn't fall clear – it fell on the rocks. And the governor was angry with us."

They went five or six more steps, then Dantes felt them take him by the head and by the feet.

"One!" said the men. "Two! Three – and away!"

Dantes felt himself thrown into the air, and then he was falling, falling. He was being drawn quickly down by a heavy weight, but it seemed to him as if he was in the air for a hundred years. At last, with a great splash he met the cold water. As he did so, he gave a cry, which was stopped at once by the water as it closed over him.

Dantes had been thrown into the sea, and he was being drawn down towards the bottom by a great stone tied to his feet.

The grave of the Chateau d'If was – the sea.

Chapter 12
The *Young Amelia*

Dantes was wise enough not to fight for air. He kept his mouth shut after that cry of surprise. In his right hand he still held the knife. He quickly cut open the bag, got his arm out, and then his body. But he could not free himself from the stone. It was pulling him down and down. He reached down, and – just as he felt that he was at the end of his strength – cut the stone free. He rose quickly to the top of the water, while the stone took down to the bottom of the sea the bag which had almost become his real grave-cloth.

Dantes drew in the night air. Then he began to swim under the water so as not to be seen.

When he came up a second time, he was nearly a hundred metres from the place where he had first fallen into the sea. He saw above him a black and stormy sky over which the wind was driving the hurrying clouds. In front of him lay the great sea – black, fearful. Behind him, blacker than the sea, blacker than the clouds, rose the Chateau d'If, like a giant of stone, its rocks like arms reaching out to take hold of him. And on the highest rock there was a lamp that lit up the forms of two men. He thought that they were looking at the sea. Perhaps they had heard his cry. Dantes went down again under the water and remained there a long time.

When he came up again, the light had gone. He began to swim out to sea.

He swam for hours, trying to reach an island. A great storm passed over the sea.

"In two or three hours," he thought, "the keeper will enter my room. He will find the body of my poor friend. He will look for me and not find me, and then he will call for help. Then the underground passage will be discovered. The men who threw me into the sea – and who must have heard my cry – will be questioned. Boats filled with soldiers will be sent out after the escaped prisoner. The great bell will sound, and everyone will be looking for a man who is wandering about without clothes, trying to find food. Soldiers will be on watch in Marseilles, while the governor and his men search for me on the sea. I am cold. I am hungry. I have lost even the knife which saved my life. Oh, my God, I have suffered enough, surely. Help me, oh help me!"

As Dantes said this prayer, with his eyes turned towards the Chateau d'If, he saw a little ship. It was coming out from Marseilles and was moving quickly out to sea.

It drew near to him. He rose up on the waves and shouted and waved his hand. The ship turned towards him and a boat was let down.

With two men in it, the boat came towards him. He began to swim to meet it. But he had used up more of his strength than he had thought. There was no power in his arms, and his legs would not move. He gave a cry. The men in the boat hurried, and one of them cried out, "Keep up! We're coming!"

The words reached his ears as a wave passed over him. He came up again, and then he felt himself go down as if the stone were still tied to his feet. The water closed over his head. The sky seemed to be red. Then someone caught him by the hair and pulled him up. And after that he heard and saw nothing.

When Dantes opened his eyes, he found that he was on board the ship. The first thing he did was to look and see where the ship was going. They were leaving Chateau d'If behind. He gave a weak cry of joy.

The captain came to see him. Dantes told him that he was a seaman who had lost his ship in the storm. The captain said that Dantes could stay on the ship if he worked.

Suddenly, the deep sound of a bell rang across the waters.

"Hey! What's that?" cried the captain.

"A prisoner has escaped from the Chateau d'If," replied Dantes.

The captain looked at him, but he looked as if he cared nothing about the matter, and the captain's fears – if he had any – died away.

"Well, even if it's him," the captain said to himself, "he'll be useful to us."

Dantes soon found out what kind of trade was done by the ship in which he was sailing, the *Young Amelia*. He heard the men talking, and he knew very soon that the *Young Amelia* was a "free-trader", that is, a ship which sets its goods on shore – on a dark night – in a bay where no customs officers come, so that they do not need to pay anything on the goods. The captain at first seemed in doubt whether he could trust Dantes or not. He wondered whether he might not be a customs officer who had told the story of the storm as a way of getting on board. In time, Dantes was able to make the captain believe in him, and by the time they reached Leghorn it was clear that his mind was quite easy about the new man.

As Leghorn, Edmond went to get his beard and hair

cut. All these years he had not seen his own face, and he wanted to see how much he had changed.

When the work was complete, he asked the hairdresser for a glass. When he entered Chateau d'If, he had had the round and open face of a young man and a happy one. There were great changes. His face was longer. His mouth was harder and stronger. His eyes were deep and thoughtful, and his skin, kept so long from the sun and open air, was whiter. Even his voice had changed. His long suffering had made it soft and rather sad.

"Even my best friend," he thought, "wouldn't know me. I hardly know myself."

After leaving the hairdresser he went to buy some clothes. Then, a changed man in dress as well as in face, he went back on board the *Young Amelia*.

The men of the *Young Amelia* served their captain well. They worked hard and wasted no time at Leghorn. The captain very soon had his ship loaded again. He had to get the goods out of Leghorn quickly, and to get them on shore at Corsica.

They set sail, and Edmond felt again the joy of the open sea, about which he had dreamed so often in prison.

Early next morning, the captain found Dantes standing at the side of the ship, looking at a great mass of rocks which the rising sun coloured with rosy light. It was the island of Monte Cristo.

Dantes thought, as they passed, that he had only to jump over the side, and in an hour he would be on the island. "But even if I did that," he thought, "how would I get the treasure away? What would the captain think? I must wait." He had learnt how to wait. He had waited for years to be free. He could wait a few months to be rich.

Edmond sees the island of Monte Cristo

And perhaps that treasure was only a dream, a child of Faria's mind. And yet there was the letter of Prince Spada. That seemed real enough. Dantes said the letter over to himself from the beginning to the end: he had not forgotten a word of it.

Night came on, and Edmond watched the island become beautiful with all the colours of evening. Then slowly it hid itself in the darkness. But he, whose eyes had been used to the darkness of a prison, continued to see it.

"How can I reach it and bring back the treasure – if there is any – safely? The treasure is mine, but I have no money to buy a small boat and get it."

He was still thinking this question over when they returned from Corsica to Leghorn. One evening, in Leghorn, the captain asked Dantes to come with him to a meeting. The captain had great trust in Dantes now, and this meeting was about a very important matter. So Edmond went with the captain to a room where all the "free-traders" used to gather together. The matter to be talked about was a ship coming from Turkey carrying silk worth a lot of money. It was necessary to find some quiet place where they could meet this ship, buy the silk, and then get it from there to the coast of France. The work had to be done in a quiet bay or on a desert island, where no customs officers would come, and no one would know anything about the business.

The captain of the *Young Amelia* thought that the best place for this would be the island of Monte Cristo. It was a desert island, and no customs officers ever went there. Indeed it seemed as if it might have been put in the sea there just for that very thing.

Hearing the name Monte Cristo, Dantes was filled with joy. They decided to start for Monte Cristo the next night.

Chapter 13
Monte Cristo

And so, by a lucky chance, Dantes was at last to reach the island, and he would reach it in such a way that no one would wonder about his reason for going there.

The sea was quiet. With a fresh wind from the south-east they sailed out. Dantes told the men that they could all go and get some sleep, and he would sail the ship. He often did this: he liked to be alone – and where can one be alone more perfectly than on a ship at night, in the silence of the great sea?

Now this silence was crowded with his thoughts, and the darkness of the night was bright with dreams.

The next evening they reached the island of Monte Cristo. The *Young Amelia* was first at the meeting place. Dantes could not wait: he was the first to reach the shore. It was dark, but at ten the moon rose over the sea, making the waves all silver.

The island was well known to the men. Dantes questioned Jacopo, the man who had saved him from the sea. "Where shall we spend the night?"

"On the ship, of course."

"Shouldn't we sleep on the island? Aren't there any caves in these rocks where one can spend the night?"

"None."

Dantes did not know what to think. Then he remembered that the opening had almost certainly been hidden by Spada, or in time it had hidden itself under fallen stones, or perhaps trees and plants had grown over it. The first thing to do was to find the hidden opening. He must wait for the next morning.

Just then a ship was seen about a kilometre out to sea. It put up some flags, to which the *Young Amelia* replied. The time had come for work.

A boat arrived and came close to the shore. Then the business began. As he worked, Dantes wondered whether he had said too much to Jacopo. "Or have the men noticed anything strange in my manner in these last few days? Might they learn about the treasure?" – No. His secret was still safe.

No one seemed surprised when he wandered away when the men were resting the next morning. He climbed high, until the men on the shore looked very small. Then he found a way cut by a stream between two walls of rock. It led him near to the place where he thought the treasure was. As he went along the coast, looking at everything with care, he thought that he saw on certain stones marks which had been made by the hand of man. Sometimes trees and plants had so grown over a stone that it was hard to tell whether it was marked or not. When he came to what he thought was the twenty-first stone, the marks ended. But there was no opening of any kind. There was just a large rock that looked so heavy that he did not think it had ever been moved.

"I must begin again," he thought. And he turned and began to go back to his friends.

During this time, the men had got a meal ready. Just as they were going to sit down and eat, they saw Dantes springing from rock to rock towards them.

Just when all eyes were on him, they saw him fall. They all ran to him, but Jacopo reached him first.

He found Edmond lying there as if dead. After some time he opened his eyes. He said that there was a great deal of pain in his knee and legs, and his head felt heavy. They wanted to carry him to the shore, but when they touched him, he gave a cry of pain, and said that he could not bear to be moved.

Of course he did not want any food, but he told the others to go and have their meal. He said that he himself only needed a little rest. "When you return," he said, "I'll feel better." They went away.

They returned an hour later. Edmond had moved about ten metres, but he did not seem to be any better. Indeed, his pain appeared to have increased.

The captain had to sail that morning. "Won't you try to get up?" he said to Dantes.

Dantes tried to do so, but each time he fell back, crying out with pain.

"He must have broken something," the captain said in a low voice. "But he's a very good fellow, and we mustn't leave him. We'll try to carry him on board the ship."

Dantes said that he would rather die than be moved.

"Well," said the captain, "it must never be said that we left a good fellow like you behind on a desert island. We won't go till evening."

This very much surprised the men, because the captain was a very hard master, and this was the first time they had ever seen him ready to lose time in this way.

But Dantes would not let rules be broken for him. "No, no," he said to the captain. "I was foolish, and I must suffer for it. Leave me a small supply of food and an axe, and the things I shall need to build myself a hut."

"But you'll die of hunger."

"I would rather do that than suffer the fearful pain of being moved."

The captain turned towards his ship, which was waiting in the bay, all ready for sea. "What are we to do?" he asked. "We can't leave you here – and yet we can't stay."

"Go. Please go," cried Dantes.

"We will be away for at least a week," the captain said, "and then we'll have to go out of our way to come here and get you."

"Well," said Dantes, "if in two or three days you see a fishing boat, ask them to come here for me. I'll pay them to take me to Leghorn. If you don't meet one, I'll be glad if you return for me."

"Listen, Captain," said Jacopo. "You go, and I'll stay and take care of him."

"And give up your part of the gains of this business to stay with me?" asked Dantes.

"Yes," said Jacopo, without any doubt.

A strange look passed over Dantes' face. He pressed Jacopo's hand. But nothing would change his wish to remain – and remain alone.

"You are a good, kind-hearted fellow," he said to Jacopo. "Heaven bless you for your kindness. But I don't want anyone to stay with me. I'll be all right after a rest."

The men left the things that Edmond had asked for, and set sail. Several times they turned round and waved to him, and Edmond replied with his hand only, as if he could not move the rest of his body.

Then, when they had gone, he said, "It's strange to find such kindness among such men."

He pulled himself up carefully to the top of the rock. From there he could see the sea. He watched the ship prepare to leave and then, like some beautiful white bird, it set out over the sea. At the end of an hour, it was completely out of sight.

Chapter 14
Treasure

Edmond climbed down from the rocks with careful steps: he was afraid that he might really fall, as he had pretended to do.

He again followed the line of marks on the stones. He noticed now that they started from a little bay, just large enough to hold a small ship such as Spada might have used. They ended at the large round rock.

"But," thought Edmond, "how could Prince Spada have lifted a rock of such weight into this place? Twenty men couldn't have done it. And if this isn't the rock, where can the place be?"

Suddenly a thought came to him. "Instead of raising it into its place, they may have let it fall!" He sprang from the rock to look at the ground above it. There were clear signs that a deep path had once been cut there, down which the rock had moved. A large stone (now almost hidden by the grass) had been placed to stop it and hold it in its present place. The holes round the edges, where the rock did not fit perfectly, had been filled in with small stones and earth.

Dantes cut away these small stones at the top, and after ten minutes he was able to put his arm into the hole. He took his axe and cut down the strongest tree he could find. He cut away the branches. Then he put one end into the hole and pulled on the other with all his strength. The rock moved. Again he pulled. The rock rose from its place, and then fell back again. Dantes rested. He gave a last pull – the greatest pull of all. The rock rose from its place. It rolled down the hill, and seemed to spring into the sea.

In the place where it had been, Dantes saw a large square stone, with a ring in the centre of it.

Dantes waited for a minute to get his strength back. Then he put the end of his tree into the ring and pressed the other end down. The stone was raised. He saw steps going down into the darkness of an underground room.

"Has anyone been here before?" thought Dantes. "Perhaps Caesar Borgia himself? But would he have wasted time putting the great rock back? I'll go down."

Instead of the darkness that he had expected to find, there was dim blue light, and the air was fresh. Both light and air entered through small holes in the rock above his head. Looking up through them, he could see the blue sky and the waving branches of trees.

After standing there for a few minutes, he could see the farthest corner of the place. There was nothing in it.

He remembered the words of the letter: "Break through into the second room." He was in the first room, and he must now find the second.

He began to strike the wall with his axe. At one place the sound seemed to be a little different. He hit it again with greater force. Then a strange thing happened. What had looked like hard rock broke and fell away easily, showing behind it a wall of square white stones. The opening had been built up and painted to look like rock.

At this point, Dantes' strength seemed to leave him. He put the axe on the ground and passed his hand across his face. He went up the steps, out into the open air. All lay quiet in the bright sunlight. He could see only a few fishing boats far away on the blue sea. He had had no food for hours, but he felt no hunger. He ate a little bread and took a drink from his jar. Then he returned. The axe

Edmond looks for the treasure

seemed less heavy. He saw that the wall in front of him was made only of stones laid one on another. He pulled them off, one by one.

At last Dantes was able to enter the second room. It was smaller and darker than the other. The air had an earthy smell. He waited a little for fresh air to find its way in. Then he entered.

There was a dark corner to the left of the opening. But to the eyes of Dantes there was no darkness. He looked round this second room. There was nothing in it.

The treasure, if there was any, must be hidden in that dark corner.

The time had arrived. When he had dug up some earth, he would learn the truth. He went to the corner and with all his strength began to dig. Suddenly his axe fell on something hard. Even the great bell of Chateau d'If had not moved Dantes' heart as that sound did. He raised the axe to strike again. Again the same sound.

"It is a great box, made of wood, with strong metal bands round it," he said at last.

Just then, a shadow passed across the entrance. Dantes took his axe, sprang through the opening, and ran up the steps. It was only a wild goat. He could see the marks of its feet. It was eating quietly among the trees on the left.

He stood in thought. Then he took a dry branch and set fire to it, and went down again. He wanted to see everything. As he drew near to the hole, he saw that he had indeed uncovered the top of a box with metal bands on it. He fixed his burning branch in the ground. Then he quickly cleared the top of the box. It was about a metre long by half a metre broad. In the centre there was a piece of silver set into the wood. There was something drawn on the silver – the mark of the Spada family.

There was no longer any doubt that the treasure was there. No one would have taken such trouble to hide a box if there were nothing in it.

He cut away the earth round the box. Then he tried to lift it. It was not possible. He tried to open it, but there was no key. He took his axe to break it open. The top came away; the wood was old and soft.

Dantes stepped back. He closed his eyes as children do when they look at the thousands of stars on a bright clear night. He opened them again – and stood as if in a dream.

The box was separated by boards into three parts. In the first part were gold coins of many different dates and countries. Most of them bore the head of Pope Alexander, the ruler of Rome at the time of Caesar Borgia. In the second part were bars of gold. From the third part Edmond took a handful of jewels. As he dropped them and they fell on one another, they sounded like winter rain on the window.

After touching, feeling, looking at these treasures, Edmond ran back to the steps like a madman. He sprang up on a rock from which he could see the sea. He was alone – alone with these unnumbered, unheard-of treasures! Was he awake – or was it a dream?

And then he became quieter. Evening was coming on. A piece of bread and a mouthful of water were all the dinner he needed. He fell asleep lying over the opening of the treasure room.

Chapter 15
At Marseilles

When daylight came, Dantes climbed to the top of the highest rock to see if there were any houses or men on the island. There were none. It was truly a desert island; hard rock, with some trees and grass only on the thin soil of the lower parts.

He returned to the treasure place, went into the second room, and took as many jewels as he could safely hide in his clothing. Then he put back the earth over the box, and put sand over the place, so that no one could see that the earth there had ever been moved. He then put a large stone over the opening and covered it with earth, and set some quick-growing plants in the earth. Then he went over the ground all round the place, hiding every footmark. When he left the place it looked as if it had never been visited.

Then he set himself to wait for the return of his friends. That was not easy. It was no joy to him to sit and watch over his great treasure. He wanted now to return to live among men, and he knew well the power that these riches would give him. Danglars, Caderousse, even Villefort, would be powerless against him now – little people not worth his thought. What good he could do with so much money! And what joy he could bring to those who were nearest to his heart!

After six days the *Young Amelia* returned. From a distance Dantes knew the shape of its sails and its way of sailing. He went down to the shore, pretending that his leg still hurt, and asked how the business had gone.

They answered that they had got the goods safely to land. But just as they had finished, they heard that a government ship had just left Toulon and was hurrying to catch them. They went off as quickly as possible, and wished that Dantes had been with them, because he could have helped them a lot. They were almost caught when luckily night came on, and they were able to turn back on their course and so get away.

They were all very sorry that Dantes should not get his part of the gains, which, they said, were large. Dantes had to stop himself from laughing.

The *Young Amelia* had come to Monte Cristo only to get him. He went on board, and the ship sailed for Leghorn.

At Leghorn, Dantes went to the house of a merchant that he knew. He sold four of his smallest stones to this merchant. Edmond was half afraid that questions might be asked at finding such jewels in the hands of a common seaman. But the merchant said nothing: he had paid for them far less than they were worth.

The next day, Dantes went to the captain and told him that his uncle, who had just died, had left him a large amount of money, and that he wished to leave the ship. The captain was sad at losing him, and did all he could to get him to stay. Dantes gave fine presents to all the men, and they wished him every possible happiness with all their hearts. To Jacopo he gave a new ship and a present of money.

After that, he left Leghorn and went to Genoa.

At Genoa he saw a boat builder trying out a beautiful little ship in the bay. It had just been built as a yacht for an Englishman. It was so small that Dantes knew he could sail it himself, alone, without help. And it was so fast that no other ship on the water would be able to catch it.

Dantes offered much more than the proper price for it, and asked the builder to let him have it with all its ship's papers. The builder did not say yes at once, but the Englishman was not expected for several months, and the man was sure he could build another yacht like it before that. So the matter was settled.

The builder offered to find seamen for the ship, but Dantes said that he needed none – that to do everything himself was, for him, the whole pleasure of sailing. But he asked the man to make a hidden place in the ship, with three separate parts in it. This might be made just at the head of his bed. The builder promised to have it ready by the next day.

The next day, Dantes sailed away from Genoa, alone. A large crowd had come to see the rich "Englishman" who always sailed his yacht himself. There were cries of wonder when they saw how perfectly the ship moved under his hand. Indeed, Dantes knew that the men of Genoa, who are the masters of shipbuilding, had never made anything so perfect.

The people followed the ship with their eyes as long as they could see it. They wondered where it was going. Some said Corsica, others said the island of Elba, others thought it might be Africa. No one thought of Monte Cristo.

It was there that Dantes sailed his yacht. He arrived there on the second day. It had covered the distance from Genoa in thirty-five hours.

Dantes had carefully noticed the line of the shore, and instead of going to the usual place, he took his ship into the little bay. There was no one on the island. No one had been there since he went away. The treasure was just as he had left it.

Early the next day, he began the work of carrying his riches on board. Before night came, the whole of the treasure was safely stored in the hidden place.

One fine morning, a small but beautiful yacht sailed into Marseilles. It tied up just near the steps from which, on that never-to-be-forgotten night, Dantes had been put on board the boat which was to take him away to the Chateau d'If.

The customs officers came on board to look at the ship's papers. A soldier stood near the steps – even now that sight sent fear into Dantes' heart.

Edmond had decided to give himself a rich man's name. He showed the officers the ship's papers that he had got at Genoa. The papers said that the yacht was owned by the "Count of Monte Cristo".

"There is no reason," said the officers, wishing to please the rich yacht owner, "why the count should not go on shore at once, if he wishes to. The papers are all in order."

One of the first men he met on shore was old Nicolas, who had served with him on the *Pharaoh*. He went straight up to Nicolas and asked him a number of questions, carefully watching the man's face. No word or look showed that Nicolas knew him. He gave him some money and turned away, but before he had gone many steps he heard Nicolas loudly calling to him to stop. Dantes turned to meet him.

"You meant," said the good fellow, "to give me a piece

of silver, but you have given me this gold coin by mistake."

"Yes, my good man," said Dantes, "I see I made a small mistake. As thanks for pointing it out to me, take this second gold coin."

The man was so surprised that he could not speak.

Dantes continued on his way. Each step he took brought fresh hopes and fears. Every tree, every street was crowded with thoughts of the past.

He went on until his father's house was in sight. At this point, the thought of his father's love made his knees feel weak, but he went on, and did not stop until he found himself at the door of the house.

He opened the door. Something white – a letter – lay at his feet. He picked it up.

"Are my eyes blind? If not, why can't I read the name? Or why can't I read it properly? It looks like 'Mercedes'. But why? I'm dreaming."

Dantes came to the door of his father's room. It was shut, but from inside he heard the sound of quietly moving feet. Then there was silence, broken by a weak cry of pain.

And then there came a voice, weak and far, like the voice of a bird lost in the darkness.

Someone answered it very gently: "Yes, soon. Very soon now. But keep quiet. You need all your strength."

Dantes put out his hand to open the door, but the hand fell back to his side, and his feet would not move from the floor.

"But I tell you he is here," said the weak voice again. "Why don't you go and call him in?"

"Try to get a little sleep now. Perhaps when you wake——"

Edmond and Mercedes

"I tell you he is here. Haven't I seen him coming up the street, seen him stand and look up at this window with his dear eyes? So changed. So changed."

"Yes, he will be changed, won't he?"

"Tell him to come quickly. Tell him that Death is waiting at my side – waiting only until I see him. Open the door, I say." The voice grew stronger with the last of life. "Open the door, I say, and bring him in!"

There were footsteps. The door opened slowly – and Mercedes stood there, dark-eyed from long watching by that bedside.

She saw him, doubted, finding him so changed, and then she fell forward with one cry, as if her heart were broken with the suddenness of too much joy. Then, taking his hand, she cried, "Come quickly so that he can see you."

The old eyes looked up at him, dim and beautiful in their last silent look of love.

The eyes closed. "Kiss me," he said. "Hold me in your arms, Edmond. – You can come now, Death."

At the return of Napoleon in 1815, Danglars had left France. He had not been seen again. It was believed that his ship was lost in a storm. Caderousse was still alive, said Mercedes, but he was very poor.

"Look," said old Nicolas to the soldier standing by the steps.

On the deep blue line which separates the Mediterranean sea from the sky, was a white sail, no larger than a bird's wing.

"He's gone," said old Nicolas, "that rich Englishman."

"Yes. I saw him go," replied the soldier. " – And her."

Questions

Questions on each chapter

1 *The ship comes home*
 1 Who was Mr Morrel?
 2 Who asked Dantes to go to Elba?
 3 Who was Mercedes?

2 *Father and son*
 1 Why didn't Edmond's father have enough money?
 2 Which two men did not like Edmond?

3 *Mercedes*
 1 What did Dantes have to take to Paris?
 2 Why did Danglars use his left hand to write the letter?
 3 Who was the letter addressed to?

4 *The judge*
 1 What did Marshal Bertrand give to Dantes?
 2 Whose name was on the letter?
 3 What did Villefort do to the letter?

5 *The prison*
 1 Where did the boat take Dantes?
 2 Who was in charge of the whole prison?
 3 How far down was Edmond's new room?

6 *Underground*
 1 Who came to visit the Chateau d'If?
 2 What did the visitor write in the prison book?

7 *Number Twenty-seven*
 1 Why did Edmond break his water pot? (He wanted . . .)
 2 How did Number Twenty-seven reach the window?
 3 How long had Faria been a prisoner in the Chateau d'If?

8 *Faria's room*
   1 What did Faria use for oil in his lamp?
   2 What did he teach Edmond?
   3 Where did Faria keep the liquid that saved his life?

9 *The story of the treasure*
   1 Why did Caesar Borgia poison Prince Spada?
   2 What appeared when Faria lit the paper?
   3 On what island was the Spada treasure hidden?

10 *The death of Faria*
   1 What did Dantes do before Faria burnt the paper?
   2 What did the keeper do when he found Faria's body?
   3 Who examined Faria's body to be sure that he was dead?

11 *The grave of the Chateau d'If*
   1 What was the "grave cloth" of the Chateau d'If?
   2 Where did Dantes put Faria's body?
   3 What was tied to Dantes' feet?
   4 What was the "grave" of the Chateau d'If?

12 *The Young Amelia*
   1 How did Dantes get free from the bag and the stone?
   2 The *Young Amelia* was a "free-trader". What did that mean?
   3 What ship did the free-traders decide to meet at Monte Cristo?

13 *Monte Cristo*
   1 What were the men doing when Dantes fell?
   2 What did the captain leave on the island for Dantes?
   3 Who wanted to stay with Edmond?

14 *Treasure*
   1 What did Dantes use to move the rock?
   2 What kind of box was the treasure in?
   3 What was in the third part of the box?

15 *At Marseilles*
   1 Where did Dantes buy a yacht?
   2 What did the boat builder add to the yacht for Dantes?
   3 Who sailed away from Marseilles with Dantes?

Questions on the whole story

These are harder questions. Read the Introduction, and think hard about the questions before you answer them. Some of the questions ask for your opinion and there is no fixed answer.

1 This book is a historical novel. Which of these people in the book were real people in history?
   Edmond Dantes; Marshal Bertrand; Napoleon; Caesar Borgia; Faria; The Count of Monte Cristo

2 Fathers and sons: Find these words in the book, and answer the questions that follow them.
   a "But, dear father, now that I have seen you and know that you have all you need, I must go and pay another visit."
      1 Who was the speaker?
      2 Where was he?
      3 Who heard the speaker's words besides the father?
      4 How did the speaker know that his father had all that he needed?
      5 Who was the speaker going to "pay another visit" to?
   b "Oh, my father, must you always stand in the way of my happiness?"
      1 Who spoke the words?
      2 Who was his father?
      3 What was his father doing?
      4 Who heard the words?
      5 What did the speaker do to try to save his own "happiness"?
   c "You are my child, born to me in this prison."
      1 Who is the speaker?
      2 Who is he speaking to?
      3 Where are they?
      4 Try to explain what the speaker meant.

3 The people in Alexandre Dumas' novels are not all either good or bad. Can you give examples to show that the following are partly good and partly bad?
   a Villefort; b the Chief Officer of Prisons; c the captain of the Young Amelia.

4 At the end of the book, where do you think Edmond and Mercedes might have sailed to?

5 Do you think the ending is right for Edmond Dantes?

73

New words

allies
countries that have joined together to fight a war

century
a hundred years in history. Example: **the seventeenth century** = the years 1601– 1700

course
the direction (or directions) a ship sails in to get from one place to another

customs
money that must be paid to a government on goods brought into the country

desert (island)
(an island) without any people

dim
without much light

grave
the hole in the ground that a dead person's body is placed in

lend
give (money, etc) to someone to use for a time

splash
the noise of water thrown up by something falling into it

yacht
a small ship or sailing boat used for pleasure